The Little Jesus of Sicily

The Little Jesus of Sicily

Fortunato Pasqualino

Translated by Louise Rozier

❋

Drawings by Ken Stout

The University of Arkansas Press

Fayetteville 1999

03   02   01   00   99   5   4   3   2   1

Designed by Liz Lester

♾ The paper used in this publication meets the minimum
requirements of the American National Standard for Permanence
of Paper for Printed Library Materials Z39.48-1984.

LIBRARY OF CONGRESS CATALOGING-IN-PUBLICATION DATA

Pasqualino, Fortunato, 1923–
[Giorno che fui Gesù. English]
The little Jesus of Sicily / Fortunato Pasqualino ;
translated by Louise Rozier.
p.   cm.
ISBN 1-55728-572-1 (cloth : alk. paper). —
ISBN 1-55728-573-X (pbk. : alk. paper)
1. Sicily (Italy)—Social life and customs—Fiction.
2. Saint Joseph's Day—Italy—Sicily—Fiction.
I. Rozier, Louise, 1952–   II. Title.
PQ4876.A88G513   1999
853'.914—dc 21   99-38364
CIP

A mon père

✳

Acknowledgments

I wish to thank Mr. Fortunato Pasqualino for his friendship and encouragement, Professor John DuVal for introducing me to the novel and for his precious advice, Professor Michele Lettieri from the University of Toronto for his support, and Professor Ken Stout for graciously lending his artistic talent and inspiration to this effort. Thanks are also due to Ms. April Brown, Dr. Hope Christiansen, Mr. Scot Danforth, and Ms. Brenda Moossy for their useful suggestions and their valuable criticism. Finally, I want to thank Franklin Evarts for sharing his life with me, and my son, Jake, for being who he is.

Contents

Translator's Preface

The Little Jesus of Sicily is an autobiographical work in which Pasqualino narrates a childhood memory to his children, creating a vibrant picture of life in a small Sicilian village shortly before World War II. The events recounted, which take place over a few days, portray a society and reality filtered through the spiritualized imagination of a very sensitive and intuitive child. The novel renews a tradition of literature found in works of regional and southern Italian inspiration and belongs to that category of rare books which are suited to please children and adults alike: Grimm's legends and fairy tales, La Fontaine's fables, Saint-Exupéry's Little Prince, or Cervantes' Don Quixote.

The Little Jesus of Sicily can be read at many different levels. On the surface it is a captivating tale. At a deeper level it is a voyage in time, an account of life in a rural Sicilian community, a reality that has almost vanished. Pasqualino ponders the loss of customs and traditions of his native village while reflecting on the impact of industrialization and modernization on society. It is possible to discern a still deeper level—a spiritual one—where Pasqualino shares his Christian beliefs without ever resorting to pious platitudes. Imagination, poetry, and faith are at the core of Pasqualino's spiritual quest as he asks simple but fundamental questions about the meaning of existence. The process of seeking and questioning is a natural one; it is an invitation to readers to reflect on greater, more universal concerns. A profound meditation on the human condition, this novel depicts in great detail the hardships and the ordinary pleasures of day-to-day life while examining the beliefs and forces that sustain people through suffering and adversity. No easy answers are proposed; however, the questioning nature of this work, as well as its imagery and its eloquence, will linger in the minds of readers. *The Little Jesus of Sicily* is a timeless tale which honors and celebrates the humanity that is within all of us, regardless of time, place, or culture.

About the Translation

I decided to translate *The Little Jesus of Sicily* for one simple reason: I fell in love with it. I started the novel and could not put it down. I saw myself in it, I saw my child, and I saw the child who resides in us all and longs for wonder. It was beautiful, it was funny, and it made me happy; I wanted to share this precious feeling of joy with other readers.

The experience of translating the novel has been very exciting and gratifying. The process involved resolving a galaxy of issues and creating a very personal partnership with the work, the author, and ultimately with the eventual readers. Time and again I was reminded that a translation is an *interpretation*. The challenges I faced stemmed from Mr. Pasqualino's good writing. I was amazed at how the seemingly simple style of the Italian narrative could be so difficult to render into

English. I knew, of course, that syntax, punctuation, and morphology have their own rules in each particular language. However, to preserve and recreate the same effect in the English narrative that the original has, I had to become keenly sensitive to the magic and power of the words themselves. My greatest struggle lay in identifying and being consistent with the two voices in the novel: the voice of Pasqualino the child and that of Pasqualino the narrator. Another difficulty related to these sometimes divergent voices was finding a rhythm in English that closely mirrored that of the Italian narrative. To capture the voices of the author and to be true to the spirit of the Sicilian mentality, I tried to select not only words that could cross language boundaries—and whose nuances and qualities reflected most accurately their Italian counterparts— but expressions that offered weight, rhythm, and musicality comparable to the Italian. I chose to leave some words and expressions in Italian and in the Sicilian dialect because of their beauty and significance. With time, a pact—a silent one— established itself between the translation and the original text as the latter was reborn and reshaped into its new form. I wanted this process to be seamless and invisible. My goal was to present English-speaking readers with Pasqualino's beautiful work *The Little Jesus of Sicily.*

About the Author

Fortunato Pasqualino was born in Butera, Sicily, in 1923. He studied philosophy and history, taught for many years in Sardinia and Rome, and worked for the RAI (Italian National Radio Network). He lives in Rome with his wife, Barbara, and

four children and writes for cultural magazines and newspapers.
He is also the author of many works of fiction, philosophical
essays, and plays. Mr. Pasqualino is the recipient of several prizes
(Campiello, 1963; Pescara, 1964 and 1978; and the Ennio
Flaiano prize for theater, 1978).

1

The Annunciation

Yes, for one day I was Jesus, the Son of God. People in Butera, Sicily, (that's where I was born), used to celebrate Saint Joseph's Day by choosing the Holy Family from among the poor children of the community. In many other villages, such as Pietraperzia, a musical band and the dignitaries of the community and the church would pick up the chosen children and take them to the town square where a big table, set for everyone, waited to be blessed by Little Jesus. That is why on that day one could see a child blessing the kneeling crowd as if he were a high priest. For the entire day, the chosen children did not answer to their given names; they were Jesus, Joseph, and Mary. People addressed them with the utmost respect as if they were praying to God and the saints. People would ask for and receive favors, and sometimes even miracles were performed, at least that's what they said in some villages. The boy Christ was given the church key. He would enter, go up to the altar, and speak sacred words, like Jesus in the Temple of Jerusalem. In Gela, the Holy Family reenacted the drama of the birth of

the Son of God amid the excitement of the faithful: again, as in Bethlehem, the doors remained shut to them as the world was unable to understand. In Butera, the celebration was more modest but no less important, especially for the one chosen to be Jesus. A great desire would well up in his soul that at last all wishes would be granted—from the simple things the world needed to the greater things it had always yearned for.

The annunciation that I was selected to be Jesus came in a clamor of cow bells to the house in the country where we lived. It was the eighteenth of March, and Tano the *curatolo,* the shepherd, brought the news with his flock of sheep, goats, and cows, along with an avalanche of sounds, soft and loud, piercing and dull, deep and gloomy, sweet and muffled. His was a strange herd of a hundred or so sheep, a dozen goats, five cows, and half-a-dozen dogs, including some strays that Saro, the *curatolo*'s nephew, kept chasing off, screaming and throwing stones but never really hurting them, or intending to. Saro was about fifteen years old. He whistled and yelled constantly, throwing rocks and hitting the animals with sticks, especially the goats, the most stubborn. Sometimes a bunch of pigs, also belonging to the herd, would follow Tano's flock. *Curatolo* means "shepherd," but a special kind of shepherd: he both owned and did not own the herd. Some of the sheep belonged to the owner of the mountain, and some of the cows belonged to the tenant farmer who was also the owner of the orange grove in the valley. Perhaps (I say "perhaps" because no one at home remembers precisely) the *curatolo* owned the goats, the pigs, and the she-ass that will play a very important role in this story.

At that time, the villagers, mainly the children, used to drink goat's milk. In the morning, the goatherds would pass through the streets and milk the goats on the spot in front of the houses. They measured the milk by counting the number of squirts they pulled from the udder. I remember the sounds, different sounds, as the warm, foaming milk filled the tureens. Some goatherds used little measuring cylinders made of metal: one-fourth of a liter, half a liter, a liter. Instead of leaving the milk itself, some goatherds left the goats tied to the rings in the walls, one goat at each door. They would come back to get the animals as soon as their morning rounds were over; they brought them back in the afternoon and took them again for the night. Thus the customers could milk their own goats or the ones given to them by the goatherds in exchange for the use of the pasture. When we lived in the village, we had a goat named Stelluccia, "Little Star." She had a white lock on her forehead.

Since the goatherds had to come and go several times during the day, they built their huts and pens as close as possible to the village. In Butera, they were found just below the walls of the city, between the cove and the caves. The goats followed mysterious trails, known only to them. In Gela, thanks to them, the door of the old buried city was discovered, along with the treasure we can still admire in the museum. Obviously, the goats were wilder and less afraid of danger than we boys were. Some goats did fall into the gullies. I remember one of them impaled itself on the forked branch of a wild fig tree. The herds of sheep and cows were kept farther down in the valley. In those days, almost no one drank cow's milk, nor was it used to make cheese. Either the calves drank it or it would be wasted. I remember seeing cows under the yoke of the plow, udders dripping all along the furrows. The cows were used only for plowing and pulling carts. Ultimately, the cows and calves would be eaten, their hides cut and sewn into shoes. Hard cheese was made with sheep's milk as was ricotta.

As Tano the *curatolo* yelled toward our house, sheep, cows, and goats stopped without a sound, the bells silent. My father went out with his gun. I, too, half dressed as I was, ran out to see what was going on. I saw the house surrounded by all those animals, and it made me happy.

"What is it, Curatolo Tano?"

"I have been instructed to notify you that tomorrow your son will be Jesus."

"Instructed by whom?"

"I was told yesterday evening in the village to tell you to send your son to church tomorrow morning."

"Are you sure that they meant my son?"

"Very sure."

My father was upset. If the choice had fallen on us, it meant people saw our family as among the poorest.

My mother came out. My father turned to her: "We aren't that poor. We've never lacked for bread. There are people who have none and don't even know how to get any. We work all this land. We have the garden. We can hunt. We have milk every morning. We have a cart with a mule. We can walk, while there are some people who can't even move."

"We are poor," my mother replied, "because we lost what we had, the land that was ours, your horse. But above all, we are poor because we have lost six children, our poor dead children. It is right for us to have Jesus; we deserve it. It's our privilege. The family where so many children die is the poorest, the most unfortunate."

Having said that, my mother invited the *curatolo* and his nephew to come in and have some cookies and wine. Hearing my mother's invitation, the animals moved toward the house. They grazed up to the front door under the shaft of the cart and along the wall of the chicken coop, scaring the chickens. A young goat even came into the house. The *curatolo* realized that this was getting out of hand and that my father did not appreciate a whole lot of familiarity from the animals. One look from the *curatolo* was enough, and the nephew, howling, throwing rocks and hitting them with sticks, drove them away from the house.

After accepting the cookies and the wine, Curatolo Tano and his nephew left with the herd. They all disappeared in a few moments as if they had grown wings and flown toward the mountain, leaving behind the lowing of the cows, the bleating of the sheep, and the clatter of the cattle-bells.

Again my father declared that we were not the poorest of the village. My mother said, "Forget about being poor. Think about the privilege, the pleasure for our son."

"I am thinking about the shame of being on the list of the poorest families and about how badly our son will feel when he is old enough to understand."

Truth be known, I already understood. I was seven years old, maybe a bit older. I could ride a horse, kill spiders, geckoes, and small snakes. I had killed a viper, thinking it was just a slow, non-poisonous little snake. But as far as my parents were concerned, I had to wait and grow a bit more to really understand. That is why they didn't care if I was listening when they talked about certain important things.

Before going any further with this story, I must satisfy my four children, Laura, Linda, Dario, and Francesco. I must answer Laura, who speaks for all of them when she asks if this story has anything to do with the life of Jesus. I say that the

Gospels are full of shepherds, herds, fields, and little villages and that the Bible is always talking about goats, sheep, and donkeys. Many of Jesus' parables had to do with wheat and grapes and also with plants and animals very similar to those in this story. But above all, it has to do with Jesus who lives in us and with us who live in Him, making His and our story one and the same.

II

Earth Is Also in Heaven

I should have mentioned the violent storms that had broken out just before my annunciation. Strong winds snapped branches and lifted the tiles from the roofs, sweeping away the haystacks like children's puppets. Torrents of rain flooded trails and dirt roads. Water fell, and the heavens rumbled. On the morning of the seventeenth, it started all over again. When the rains finally stopped, it looked as if the sea had met the sky, and the horizon was about to dissolve and become one with all the waters that ran over the earth and around it. That same afternoon, the "eye of the goat"—a sure prelude to a rainbow—appeared on the other side of the mountain between the clouds. The eye of the goat was a clear, deep blue gash across the gray sky with a cirrus cloud in the middle of it, like a big pupil. My father showed it to me. It did look like the big eye of a goat, eyebrows and all. The eye took in the whole countryside in its sunny glance. A donkey brayed.

"The worst is over, but let's not be too sure," said my father.

Tano the *curatolo,* on the other hand, was sure enough to bring his herd to the new pastures on the mountain the next day. So it was thanks to the eye of the goat that the news was announced by the ringing of cow bells and not by the musicians and the town crier's drum. The *curatolo* was proud to come visit with his noisy troupe and took great satisfaction in telling us that only the best bells hung from the necks of his animals. Everyone could hear them. What he truly wanted us to know (without saying so) was that he could go anywhere with his head high, proudly, and that his herd was well-behaved. Truth be told, after the *curatolo* left, my father took my mother and me to the path leading to our vegetable garden and showed us the prints left in the mud by the goats and pigs belonging to none other than the *curatolo*'s herd itself. But the few unruly young animals that eluded the boy's supervision—through no fault of his own—caused no damage, and my father smiled.

"Do you believe in the eye of the goat?" my mother asked my father.

"Why not? Tano, the *curatolo,* believes in it!" my father replied, amused.

✳

Taking advantage of the sunny day, my mother took me with her to wash clothes. I would help her spread the sheets between the sour cherry trees that grew around the *gebbia.* The *gebbia* was a big tub in which the water from a spring was collected and used during the summer to water the orange trees and the vegetable garden.

"Do you know that tomorrow you will be Jesus?"

My mother's words hit me. Like all children, I knew that Jesus had been born in a cave, and it made sense to me, since in those days, people's houses looked a little like the cave in Bethlehem. The rooms were big and dark. Attached to the house there was a manger and a stable with a donkey, and a mule . . . and perhaps a horse, a cow, chickens, and rabbits. In a way, we all felt that we had been born in a cave. I knew that from the day he was born, Jesus was persecuted by Herod; I could understand that, too, after hearing the adults repeat that our own king wanted to kill all the children as soon as we were born. He wanted our deaths at all costs, and he would dispatch guards in disguise to spread diseases and fatal illnesses among us (figments of people's imagination, of course). If he could not kill us with plagues and calamities when we were young, he would wait for us to grow up, take us from our families, and send us to kill and to be killed in his wars. I knew that, in a way, each one of us was Christ, or more exactly a "poor Christ," as the most unfortunate were called. But I also heard over and over that in the end Jesus Christ was victorious and had overcome evil and death. How could this be? I asked myself. People still got sick and kept on dying. "It is because of our sins!" the preaching friars explained. But the sin of all sins, Adam and Eve's sin, hadn't it been absolved? I thought that at least people who had been baptized and attended mass should not get sick and die.

At that time, people in the villages lived by images and sayings from the Bible. If a woman was in deep mourning, people would refer to her as the Virgin in Sorrow. Men with exceptional strength were called Samsons. Every man who was over six foot tall was Goliath, the giant, and all the short ones felt like David in comparison. A traitor was called Cain or Judas. A Pilate was anyone who, washing his hands of responsibility, refused to get involved. There were very few Bibles, and often people could not even read them, and yet the Holy Scriptures spilled into our lives, into our emotions, vices, and virtues. Every road had crosses, votive chapels, sanctuaries. You could not find a spring that did not have its divine revelation.

When my mother asked if I knew that I would be Jesus, it was not because she thought I needed religious instruction to know who Jesus was. Indeed not! She assumed I knew. It would have been like teaching me how to breathe or walk. She started washing the clothes, and singing:

> You were born like the sun,
> Sun of thousands of rays.
> My head is spinning round and round . . .

I don't remember what comes after that. I just remember the sun and its thousands, millions, billions, an infinite number of rays. After the downpour of the preceding days, the country- side sparkled as if made of mirrors and crystals. The sun in the water of the *gebbia* shone on the washboard, glistening in the soapy foam and through my mother's fingers. The light was all around us: on the foliage of the trees, on the valley, on the mountains. It was like the omnipotent God of Sunday school: in Heaven, on Earth, and everywhere else.

A cloud hid the sun and everything faded away. "Oh no! Please don't," said my mother. "Blessed cloud, why did you have to hide the sun right now? Let me dry the sheets."

As soon as she spoke, the cloud went away, spreading its coat of shadows towards the woods, away from us. The sun returned on the sheet spread between the sour cherry trees, and on everything else.

"Mother, you told the cloud to leave and the cloud left."

"The cloud was supposed to leave, and it left on its own. What I said had nothing to do with it."

"But I bet it heard you."

"You really are a little child, my son."

We were spreading the small pieces of laundry on the briars.

"Mother, is the sun there at night?"

"Sure."

"Where is it?"

"In the heavens. The sun, the moon, the stars, the planets, and even the Earth."

"The Earth? But the Earth is where we are now!"

"Yes dear, but the Earth we're on is also spinning in the heavens."

Now it was my head that was spinning. I asked more questions.

"What was Jesus like when he was a child?"

"Like all the other children. When people are little, they are all alike. There is no Son of God, or son of poor people. The differences come later."

"Did Jesus play?"

"Of course."

"What was his favorite game?"

"I don't know."

"Was Jesus sick sometimes?"

"No, I don't think so."

"Well, at least he had malaria, didn't he? They must have had mosquitoes even then."

"Yes, but mosquitoes didn't hurt him. They couldn't hurt him."

"He knew he was Jesus?"

"He knew he was a child, and that's all."

Afraid she had hurt my feelings, my mother added, "We know that Jesus was born in a cave. We know that when he was twelve years old, he debated with wise men and rabbis, and his intelligence and knowledge amazed them. We do not know about his games and his toys or the other things you are asking me about. Jesus was always like a man even when he was a little boy."

"He never made mistakes, did he?"

"He could not make mistakes. Although at times he must have been impulsive like all children. Like the day, for example, when he wanted to pick figs out of season. You did the same, remember, that day in February when you went to the vineyard on the Pojo looking for grapes. But we must remember that Jesus said that the Kingdom of God was for those who have the hearts of little children."

I knew that one day, hungry and thirsty, Jesus must have gone looking for figs when they were out of season. Angry, he cursed the fig tree, making it dry up on the spot. We country kids understood such things. Every fruit ripens at the appropriate season: apples, pears, and grapes between summer and fall; oranges in winter; and cherries in spring. But one day when I was really little, I wanted grapes, and I decided to go to the Pojo and get some. I imagined the grapes hanging in big bunches from the vines, beautiful and ripe, like during the harvest. I walked and climbed a steep, stony path, tearing my pants in the briars that closed off the vineyard. What a disappointment! The vines were dry, dead, and brown. Where were the leaves, and the grapes? I cried and cried, all alone. I returned home, my eyes red and swollen. Angry, I took it out on my father and my mother as if they were the ones who had cut the leaves and taken the grapes, pressed them, and put them into the casks.

"Right now, grapes, like figs, are asleep," explained my father.

"They're asleep?"

"Yes, asleep. Spring will awaken them slowly. First they will grow buds, and then the tiny new leaves will appear . . ."

At that precise moment, surrounded by the laundry laid out to dry, I thought about it, and I noticed, pushing through the cracks of the *gebbia,* that the spiky little buds on the sucker of a wild fig tree had not yet opened.

"If Jesus knew it all, he should have known that the fig trees were asleep."

"He did, but Jesus pretended he didn't know many things so as to be more like us."

That confused me. But I thought, "Tomorrow I will be Jesus. Tomorrow I will explain it to myself."

III

Jesus Is Slapped

In those days people were not as respectful toward children as they are today. All day long children were scolded, hit and cursed by mothers and fathers . . . even by perfect strangers. The streets, dirty with dung, garbage, insects, and vermin, echoed with the shouts and screams of angry women, the swearing of men, and the cries of children. Animals were mistreated, too. Dogs could not bark without being kicked and struck with sticks and stones until they ran away, yelping, limping, and writhing from pain. On the slightest pretext, cats were hurled into the air and thrown outside the village walls, landing in the smoking ravine below where the garbage dumps were always burning. There was no joy for the asses either. The poor donkeys could not bray without being kicked and hit on their heads with belts until they stopped. In the villages, the ideal scapegoat was the mule because, except for a few instances of eccentric willfulness, like when someone refuses to take a bath or wash his hair, it usually kept silent. It showed no signs of love or happiness and never complained about the blows it received.

Even the playfulness of the lambs and the kids on their way to be slaughtered was not tolerated. Their innocence was a source of irritation, an indication that they were too stupid to know their fate.

But above all, grown-ups could not bear the sight of children having fun. They would accuse us of not knowing what life was all about; any sign of happiness was seen as a sin, and they had no peace until they spoiled it for us. Seeing us play in the street, they would call those of us too young to work names like "wasted-bread," "stolen-bread," or "treacherous bread-eaters." In the evening, the men returning from the fields would hit us with their reins without even getting off their mounts. In the few schools, rods were always kept on the teachers' desks. One teacher had a long stick leaning against the wall—like the ones used to beat down the almonds—to reach the students in the back rows. Sometimes when the grown-ups quarreled, they would take it out on us. They felt that children were always up to no good and deserved whatever abuse they got.

My parents treated me well, but they were an exception. I did, however, get my share of spankings and scoldings. In fact, I was slapped, not by my father or mother, but by a drunk, the evening before I was going to become Jesus. It happened at the tavern of the Piano della Fiera where my father had stopped to greet his friends and have a glass of wine with them.

My father and his friends were drinking to their own health when a white cat, running away from the innkeeper, jumped on the table and spilled a wine jug, splashing its red contents on the face of a customer. I laughed. The man got up, slapped me, and spitefully knocked the jug to the floor. I cried and went to my father for protection. The room got totally quiet; only my sobs could be heard. Then my father slapped me, too, but it was as if he were slapping the other man. He called the innkeeper and ordered another jug of wine. The jug was brought immediately. My father took the jug, placed it directly in front of the man who had slapped me, and said harshly, "Drink!"

The man's glazed eyes looked into my father's.

"Drink," repeated my father.

He obeyed and gulped the wine down; then he laughed with scorn.

"Bring another one!" ordered my father loudly, but his friends begged him to stop since the man was already drunk and unable to stand. The other customers said that he had started drinking long before the cat knocked over the wine.

On our way back home on the mule cart, neither of us said a word. My father broke the silence first.

"Forgive me," he said. "I had to do it. You know that my slap wasn't directed at you, don't you?"

"Yes, but I am the one you slapped. It was the cat's fault, not mine. What did I do wrong?"

"You laughed, and the man got embarrassed. Come now, stop crying or God knows what your mother will think. Besides, aren't you going to be Jesus tomorrow? Well, Jesus also got slapped and spat at, through no fault of his own."

I don't need to describe the great sense of justice and revenge that we children felt on the day when one of us was Jesus and we were surrounded by Joseph and the Virgin Mary, the apostles, and the saints. No one could touch us unless, of course, they wanted to kiss our hands and feet and beg us for forgiveness and mercy for their sins. On that day, women, who just a few days before had thrown big basins of dirty water at

us and spoiled our games, would open their arms and fall on their knees in front of us. The people who had cursed at us were either nowhere to be found or became our most faithful followers. On that day they called themselves sinners and beat their chests with their fists and with stones. This happened in many villages, and if in Butera people were less dramatic, they were just as devout.

Because I was still feeling the sting of the slaps on my face and the wounds in my pride, I was tempted to become a Jesus of the Apocalypse, a Jesus of the end of the world, a Jesus of the Last Judgment. First of all, I decided, I would make that drunkard die that very night. I was thinking about punishing my father also, just a little, perhaps a low-grade fever and the runs. Then, I would sink Butera. I would make it disappear between the valleys and fall into the sea. But first I would have to save my playmates and their parents because I wanted them to know that they were being punished: "If I destroy the village, and if everyone dies, no one will know why I did it," was my reasoning, and of course, people had to know, or what was the use? Besides, according to my fanciful imagination, I would rebuild the village later, much to the awe of all the villagers, now happy and good. Thanks to me the village would be even better than before.

Pointing to the Temple of Jerusalem, Jesus had said to the apostles: "Do you see this temple? I can destroy it and rebuild it in three days."

I remembered that Jesus said three days—no more, no less. In those three days that it would take me to destroy Butera, I would tell the people to set up camp around our house in the country. I would multiply bread and fruit and awaken the grapevines and figs, ordering all the trees to bear plentifully right then and there.

The sun was setting over the mountain, and like Joshua in the story I had heard, I tried to stop its course. The sun did not obey, and that meant I was not yet Jesus and my time had not come. The sun tipped behind the mountain and suddenly dusk settled in.

"We had better set a light on the cart. It will be dark when we arrive and we don't want the police to fine us," said my father.

He got down to light the lantern that was hanging between the wheels of the cart.

"The mule sees even when there is no moon," he said, "but the law is the law."

IV

Miracles

When grown-ups read in the Gospels "In my name you will be able to expel demons, speak in tongues, and handle snakes. If you eat something deadly or poisonous, you will not be harmed; you will heal the sick by laying your hands on them," they understand that these are figures of speech used for higher teachings. Adults do not rush to believe that they will be able to speak in different languages without having learned them first. They stay away from snakes, vipers, and other venomous reptiles. They are careful not to eat harmful food or drink deadly beverages. When the Gospel says, "If you have faith in me, you will tell the mountains 'Move!' and the mountains will move," adults don't really believe that they can make it happen.

On the other hand, a child believes it all, or at least he fantasizes about it. I thought, "Tomorrow, if I see a black snake, one of those dangerous ones, I will grab it and wear it around my neck, like a necklace. That will scare everyone. I can even touch vipers if I want. Fleas, flies, hornets, and mosquitoes won't be able to do anything to me. I won't catch malaria."

That evening during supper, even though I was not entirely interested in moving mountains, I decided to ask my mother about it.

"Is it true that someone like Jesus can move mountains?"

"Yes, but Jesus, who could do anything he wanted, left the mountains and valleys where they were."

"But he said that the mountains can be moved."

"He did say that, but he didn't move any. It wasn't necessary. Jesus worked on the essentials only."

"He made the blind see, the crippled walk, and he brought back the dead."

"Yes. But more important than anything else, Jesus loved us, and He taught us how to love and how to be good. Tomorrow, that is exactly what you have to tell everyone in church: to love God and to love one another."

"But I should perform a little miracle, don't you think?"

"Don't get any strange ideas, my son. Oh, it would be wonderful to perform all the miracles you want. But Jesus did not come to Earth to perform miracles and to free us from sacrifices and suffering. Just the opposite—Jesus said, 'He who wants to come with me should take up his own cross and follow me.' This means that each one of us must make sacrifices, drink his share of the bitter cup, and accept his own Calvary. But let's forget about such sad thoughts. Tomorrow is a day to celebrate, it is your feast day. You will choose the apostles. The priest will give you the church key, and you will walk up to the altar. From there, you will turn, face the people, and speak. Well, not exactly 'speak.' You will say few words only, pretty much what they tell you to say. Or you may be allowed to say

something on your own. If that's the case, you should pronounce God's words only, the words you remember from the
Gospels and Sunday school. A few years back, a little boy
started reciting a poem he had learned in school. People
laughed because it had nothing to do with religion. Mary and
Joseph will be waiting for you outside the church. Together,
you will go to the Castle where a big table has been set. Bless
everyone who asks you and also the people who don't ask.
God's grace should fall on all of us, especially on those who
need it most. Don't pick your nose and don't wipe it on the
back of your sleeve. Don't drink from the pitcher. Use a glass.
Remember to always eat with a spoon or fork."

My mother urged me to be a "clean" Jesus, which in Sicily
meant so many fine and beautiful things . . .

While my mother instructed me about the various tenets
of good manners, I kept thinking about the possibility of performing a miracle. I asked, "The day a person is Jesus, if he lays
his hands on a sick person, will the illness go away and the person get up?"

"Stop this nonsense, son. Forget these ideas."

But my head was full of such ideas, and it was spinning
once again, like the sun of a thousand rays my mother sang
about while washing clothes at the *gebbia*.

"A miracle would be nice, of course, but it is best not to
think about it. Go to bed. Tomorrow you will have to get up
early."

"Mother, won't you and Papa come with me?"

"No, we can't. You know that. Tomorrow you are not our
son, your father's and mine, but the son of the Holy Virgin and
God, as we really all are. Tomorrow, your father and I are two
ordinary people to you, like friends or brothers."

"His brothers? No, his children, better yet!" joked my father, meaning that my mother was exaggerating.

"That's exactly right," my mother insisted. "Tomorrow we will be his children because he represents God on Earth."

"You and Papa will be my children?"

Like my father, I did think that my mother was exaggerating a little, but I didn't mind. Actually, I liked the idea.

I thought, "I will not tell the mountains to move. I am not interested in speaking in new tongues. I don't care about touching and playing with poisonous snakes. I won't chase any demons away; I have never seen any and besides I don't know where to find them. I will be careful; I will not pick and eat mushrooms. But there is one thing I really want to do: I want to heal someone, like Nico, who is always sick. I will lay my hands on him and say, 'You are healed.' And he will be healed."

In those days, too many children got sick and died, three or four in each family. In our family, six had died before I was born: four little girls and two little boys. A couple of them died from scarlet fever, some from lethal malaria, and others from a killer flu, the so-called Spanish flu (people thought it came from Spain but in reality it came from China). Simple pneumonia would kill grown-ups and children alike. We lacked doctors and medicine, and often they could do little or no good anyway. Nowadays, even children who play doctor have a stethoscope and know how to use it. In those days, the doctors were not even aware of its existence. When the first stethoscopes arrived, they were passed around like an oddity, more to look at than to use.

Because doctors and medicine were scarce, people always called upon the saints and God to heal their children, themselves, their animals, and their crops. During the patron saint days, one could see endless lines of penitents praying to the saints, the Virgin Mary, and Jesus Christ. Some worshipers crept along the road with chains around their necks, wrists, and ankles. Some wore garments of brambles, others, crowns of thorns. Barefoot and carrying candles, they prayed and sang mournful hymns, all of them, adults and children alike.

The little girls were dressed for prayers according to the saint of the day. Tuesday was Saint Anthony of Padua's day, and they wore a brown frock with a white rope and a hood. Wednesday was the day of our Lady of Carmel, and they wore a pleated, light-brown dress made up of a simple skirt and bodice with a white and brown rope. Thursday was Saint Rita of Cascia's day (believed to be the saint of the impossible, capable of performing extraordinary miracles), and the girls wore a black tunic with a white bib. Friday was Saint Francis of Paola's day. He was a performer of great miracles who even brought a baby goat back to life and summoned it, unhurt and bleating, out of the oven where a gang of bricklayers had been roasting it. On that day the girls wore a black habit with CHARITAS inscribed in gold letters in the front, and a rope around the waist. Finally, Saturday was the Virgin Mary of the Immaculate Conception's day, and the girls wore a simple pale blue dress with a white and light-blue rope. Sunday and Monday, we rested. The boys had to wear ropes; all sorts of religious medals and crucifixes; garments in honor of our Lady; pieces of cloth with prayers, embroidered signs and symbols sewn inside their jackets; green, yellow and red ribbons; and more medals around their necks and wrists, all for their patron saints.

I did not have to wear all that stuff, thank God. My penance was to wear earrings like the Gypsies. A fortuneteller from Gela called Donna Filippa had predicted the day and the time of my birth: November 8, 1923, at 4:30 in the afternoon. According to my mother and our neighbors, during the first months of my life I confused night and day. I would sleep the entire blessed day and wake up in the evening. Nothing could make me go back to sleep. I cried all night long. My mother made a vow to Saint Rocco, Butera's patron saint. She promised that she would undress me and give him my clothes on the sixteenth of August, his saint day. She also promised to donate five liras in his name every year from then on, until she died.

In those days, newborn babies were swaddled—wrapped and bundled up in blankets like little mummies before being laid down in their cradles. In Sicily, cradles were called *nache,* and they hung like little hammocks above the marriage beds. So there I was, above my parents' heads, where I was supposed to sleep and let everyone else sleep, but I didn't. I finally got things straight on the day my mother undressed me and gave my clothes to the patron saint as he was being carried through the streets. From then on I slept at night and stayed awake during the day. I stopped crying. Would you like to know the real reason? It was because from then on I was no longer swaddled, and I was finally able to breathe! But who would dare suggest that it was not God's grace? Better yet, it was a miracle! And I do believe it was a miracle because on that day my parents got some sense, and I was no longer wrapped in hot and uncomfortable garments. In southern Italy, there was—and still is—the very bad custom of believing that babies are always cold. That is why they are always covered and bundled up, even during the summer months. And I thank Saint Rocco for taking away the blankets, wraps, and swaddling clothes that were torturing me.

During those days, the fortuneteller from Gela came back to visit us. My parents often gave her gifts and food, and she was fond of my family. On one particular day, she was sitting outside, with me in her arms. Seeing one of the gold earrings she was wearing, I grabbed it and pulled. A little streamlet of blood dripped down her cheek. My mother was upset.

"It's all right, don't worry. It's a sign of luck and greatness," said the fortuneteller with a smile. "There is one thing, however: from now on, this little lad will have to wear earrings."

And as she was talking, she removed the other gold loop and gave it to my mother. My mother was confused and protested that men, except for a few older ones, no longer wore earrings, and nobody ever wore more than one. The fortuneteller said that I did not have to wear them every day. I should only wear them for two novenas a year, in devotion to the Lady of the Chain.

Probably the fortuneteller made all this up right then and there to punish me. She probably thought, "This kid ruined my ear. It serves him right. He can wear earrings for the rest of his life. That will teach him."

It is also very possible that the penance of wearing earrings did not displease our Lady. In truth, I only wore them a few times, but that was enough to make me feel as if they were always there.

The night before Saint Joseph's Day, I had a dream. I dreamed that the dead in the cemetery were coming back to life. I was on a train, riding on a very high overpass like the ones built today but which were, in those days, only figments of our imagination. The train was pulling forty cars of toys and sweets. In my dream, it was like All Souls' Day, which in Sicily was like the Epiphany and was celebrated on November 2. Early that morning, the children would search their houses to find the gifts and the sweets brought and hidden by the Dead during the night: cookies made of carob, dry figs, sugar figurines, little clay whistles, rifles, drums, candies, and toys. These treats were called (and continue to be called in some villages) *cose di morti,* "things of the Dead," without any scary or morbid associations intended. When people enjoyed a big surprise, a visitor, or something unexpected, they used to say (and still do), "To whom do I owe it? Should I thank the Dead?" As if real surprises could only come from the other world. Later that morning, we would take our new toys and go to the cemetery with our parents. The adults went in their mourning clothes to cry and pray for the departed, and the children in their Sunday clothes to have fun and play, shoot their guns, and hide among the tombs. I remember how that surprised a preaching friar from Northern Italy. He even mentioned it in one of his sermons, "What a strange contradiction: on one side I see suffering and tears, and on the other, happiness and celebration. I wonder who is right. The adults' mourning and sorrow or the joy of the little children. I believe the truth that frees us points to the children, to their games and happiness."

It was probably some memory from All Souls' Day that made me dream about the Resurrection. In many ways, the dream was only a continuation, on a grand scale, of the games we could have played with new toys and forty train cars full of gifts—toys and gifts that could have been multiplied, if necessary. In my dream, it was also Christmas and Easter combined, and many more holidays. Finally, I saw my brothers and sisters constantly remembered and mourned by my mother. We had no pictures nor portraits of them, and I did not know what they looked like. In my dream, they were like any children. I was never photographed either, and I would be hard-pressed to tell you what my own face looked like. That may be why I feel I can see and recognize myself in the faces of many little boys.

V

The Departure

The following morning was March 19. My mother came
to my room to wake me up. It was barely dawn.

"Jesus, my Lord, please get up. It's time. The bells are ringing in the village."

Hearing my mother call me "Jesus" and "my Lord" was like
leaving one dream—the one where the Dead were coming
back to life—and entering another one, where all people's
wishes and desires could come true. But those thoughts and
perhaps even more beautiful ones vanished, chased away by
the heaviness of waking too early and having to get up. At that
moment I felt numb and a little cold. I heard the bleating of a
lamb. I ran outside to see what was going on. It was Saro slash-
ing the throat of a lamb that he held between his legs. I watched
while Saro put the bloody knife in his teeth to free his hands
and let the blood of the poor animal, not quite dead yet, drain
into a bowl. Then he cut open the stomach and removed the
entrails. He gave the skinned lamb to my mother and kept the
entrails, which he would use to curdle milk and make cheese.

It was not the first time that I had witnessed such a scene. Country children routinely saw lambs, kids, calves, colts, mules, and asses being born. Every day, they watched the animals play, mate, fight, and die. Grown-ups didn't worry about what kind of bad effect such sights might have on children. They thought children should get used to them, that's all.

I have told you about the shepherds who distributed the milk in the villages, leading their goats and milking them in front of each house. In addition to this custom, the shepherds used to skin the animals, the goats or lambs, under the eyes of the people they sold or gave them to.

We children would have preferred for the shepherds to wait a little before butchering them, a few days at least, so we could play with them. But that would have been like going to the store today and asking to buy lettuce with its roots attached so we could take it home and plant it in our own gardens. Grown-ups have their own way of looking at things. When a child sees a lamb, the first thing he wants to do is play with it, give it food and water, and take it to its pen. A child wants to take care of it. Left to his own devices he would even sleep with it at night! Grown-ups are different. Their first thought is how to eat it all up. They see the lamb right there on their plates, skinned, baked, roasted, and steaming. In their minds, the lamb is already butchered, cut and sliced, all of it, down to the very last cutlet. Nature, trees, and many other things have different meanings to different people. Some people, when they look at a tree, see how much fruit the blossoms will bear, how much of that fruit will be sold, and at what price, regardless of how beautiful the flowers or the fruit of the whole tree is. Of course, when children look at a tree, they think of picking the fruit and flowers, too, and especially of climbing the tree. I am convinced that when a child sees a pheasant, a rabbit, or a deer, the thought of killing it and eating it does not enter his mind. When my son Dario realized where the veal cutlets he liked so much came from, he pushed his plate away and said, sobbing, "What are you doing to me? Why are you making me eat animals?"

He was still little when this happened. With time, he resigned himself to the grown-up way of looking at things.

The fact that Saro knew how to skin a lamb meant that he was not a child anymore. It meant that he no longer played.

The lamb was part of a deal between Tano the *curatolo* and my father. In exchange for a few lambs, some cheese and milk, my father let the shepherd graze his herd on our fields after the harvest. Tano could also help himself to the vegetable garden whenever he wanted.

The land was not ours; we rented it. The owner provided the land, my father the labor. Both my father and my mother complained that in the end the owner did not take half the harvest, as would have been right, but three-fourths of it and sometimes even more. Also, since everything belonged to him, land and buildings alike, the owner claimed the entire fruit harvest, all the olives, the oranges, and the almonds.

"The laws, my son," my mother would tell me, venting her frustration when my father got tired of the subject, "are made against the poor. They favor the landowners, and the most dishonest ones at that. According to them, we shouldn't even lift our eyes to the branches of a tree; we shouldn't touch a single medlar, let alone an apricot or an apple. Do you know what they do to the goats and cows that graze in a field where there are trees? They tie their heads to their left front legs to keep their mouths down in the grass. The landowners would like to do the same to us. When God created Heaven on Earth, He did not keep all the trees for Himself. He kept one, the Tree of Eternal Life. He forbade Adam and Eve to eat the fruit of one tree only, the Tree of Knowledge. The landowners demand more from us than our Heavenly Father. Why, they don't even let us pick up the sorb apples!"

But at home, we ate fruit of all kinds. When it came to forbidden trees, I suspect that my father and mother were more disobedient than Adam and Eve.

What with the butchering of the lamb and my thoughts about man and nature, I forgot to tell you about the she-ass Saro brought with him. It belonged to the *curatolo*'s herd, and it was to take me to the village, like Jesus on Palm Sunday. On my way there, I was also supposed to choose the apostles, or at least a few of them, since some would already be waiting for me in front of the church. Mules, horses, and donkeys were usually very familiar with the paths and dirt roads that led to and from the village and the houses in the country. They knew the way from the homes to the water wells and springs where the jugs and demijohns they carried were filled with water. The *curatolo*'s she-ass had the reputation of being the wisest of all the mounts in Butera. But that's not all . . .

Pointing to the she-ass waiting for me under the Carob tree, my mother said, "Son, when you were three years old, this she-ass saved your life. You got terribly sick with the typhus. Your hair fell out. We were already mourning you when suddenly this she-ass—sent by God, that's what I always say—appeared. You drank her milk, and she saved your life."

I knew about my wet nurse, the she-ass. My mother told the story all the time, along with the story of the fortuneteller from Gela who foretold the day of my birth. She told of the earring I tore, and of the fame and fortune—which we were still waiting for—that should have befallen us. The story of the she-ass was for anyone who would listen; and that morning, it was for Saro. But Saro's work was done, and after pretending to listen to a few sentences, he said that he had to run because his pigs were left unattended on the river bank.

"Go on, then. Hurry! Or they'll be tearing up the ground and rooting animals from their dens, and snakes and vipers will be the only ones to thank you!" said my mother, with the tone of voice of someone who was really thinking, "Get out of here, you brat. Leave since you don't know how to listen politely."

The pigs made me think of the parable of the prodigal son, the young man who asked his father to give him his share of his inheritance and went off to the city to have fun. Once he had spent it all, he had no choice but to work as the caretaker of a herd of pigs or starve. He even had to fight with the pigs for the acorns on the ground! He thought about going back home to his father, who was rich and who spent all his time tormenting himself and longing for his son's return. When the son went back, in rags and starving, his father embraced him and ordered the servants to kill the fatted calf to celebrate his return.

For me, Saro might have been the prodigal son. I asked him why he did not go back home since his father was waiting for him.

"My father? I went to his place in Mazzarino two weeks ago. I brought him a wheel of cheese and half a lamb. If I didn't think about him, he would be left to die like a dog. When my sister was there, she tied his shoes for him, but now she is gone."

Saro spoke to my mother as if she had asked the question.

He said that his father had only one arm, the left one, and that he had lost his right arm during the war. He got a little pension from the government, but it was not enough to live on. After his daughter left, the poor man wore his shoes unlaced, like prisoners do. Now, the only time the old man had the pleasure of having his shoes tied was when Saro came for a visit and tied them for him.

I was confused. Had the parable of the prodigal son changed? How could this be? Now it was the son who brought his father gifts and tied his father's shoes?

My father came and said, "Are you still here? What are you waiting for?"

He picked me up, put me on the she-ass and added, "We know how good you are at mounting and dismounting. You do it very well. But today stay on. The she-ass knows the way; she'll get you there. All you have to do, right before you get to the village, is pull on the reins slightly, to the left, she'll know to take you to the church. By that time you'll probably have met and named some of the saints and apostles."

Worried, my mother asked, "Are you sure that the she-ass won't be bitten by the flies?"

My father smiled, "The flies are not biting yet. You ought to know that. You should know that flies bite cows in May, sheep in June, and only in July do they bite horses, mules, and donkeys. But you'll never learn, even if you spend your whole life living in the country!"

This was no ordinary fly they were talking about, but a kind of horsefly that drives cattle and horses crazy. When bitten, mules and especially the asses stop suddenly and furrow the ground with their noses, bucking and dragging along whatever is on their backs, things and people alike. The villagers talked about what had happened to an old man one day as he was riding down the mountain on his donkey. He was about to light his pipe when the flies attacked. The donkey stopped, stuck its muzzle on the ground, and bucked, throwing off the old man, pipe and all. Well, at least he did not die.

When stung, horses and mules lift their upper lip and laugh a satanic laugh. Sheep huddle up or line up single file, each with its muzzle buried in the wool of the sheep in front of it. But cows act the strangest: as soon as the flies bite them in their most sensitive parts, they break into a run, tails up and waving, and get lost along the river banks, in the cane thickets, and in the fields. Shepherds and farmers were careful not to bring their animals to pasture or anywhere else during the hottest hours of the day when the flies were the most active. If the trip was unavoidable, the animals' mouths were tied shut with supple branches and covered with big kerchiefs.

"Jesus knew all these things?" I asked.

"As the son of a carpenter, perhaps he didn't, but as the Son of God he knew these things and many more. Now go, and God bless you."

"Mother, you forgot that I am Jesus. When you woke me up you said, 'Wake up my Lord.' Now you are not calling me 'my Lord' anymore."

"You are right, forgive me. I am so used to your being my son that I forgot today you are the Son of God. Even the Virgin Mary, I am sure, must have forgotten at times that Jesus was Jesus."

VI

Temptations

Now that I was Jesus, riding alone to Butera on the she-ass, I gave free rein to all the fantasies my mother had urged me to forget. Strange ideas came to my mind, such as making the she-ass talk. Didn't a she-ass speak in the Bible? It was the one who belonged to the diviner of the Land of the Two Rivers, the man who went to curse God's people but blessed them instead. What about my mother? Didn't she say that we should think of the she-ass (whose milk had saved my life!) as sent by the Lord? What about when people want to say that an object or an animal is perfect, don't they say, "All it needs is to speak"? My she-ass was blessed; she carried Jesus, not some ordinary human being. She had to say something. So, wanting to save time, I started asking a few questions.

"How old are you? I hear that you are quite old by now." No answer.

"They call you *a scecca du curatulu,* the shepherd's ass, but what is your real name?"

Silence.

"Do you know that today I am Jesus?"

The she-ass seemed to be immersed in her own deep thoughts. Could it be that since she had not been baptized and did not go to Sunday school, she could not understand religion? But God is everywhere. Surely He was in her big, thick brain also.

"I am telling you, if I order you to speak, you must do it!"

The she-ass looked as if she understood.

I went on: "I know which way you want to take me, but we'll take a different one. We won't go by Piano della Fiera; we'll go by the cemetery instead. I'll show you what I can do."

If people had seen me talking to the she-ass, they would not have been surprised at all. Farmers and shepherds used to walk along with their animals speaking aloud to them. This happens also in the cities where people can be seen and heard talking to dogs, cats, birds, and even to worms and flowers. You see, animals and things don't answer. They keep quiet. And their silence is very soothing to anyone who always wants to be listened to and never interrupted or disagreed with.

The miracle of bringing the dead back to life was just too big. I should practice with something smaller, an ant for example. I thought, "I'll get off, look for an ant, kill it and bring it back to life. No. First I must make the she-ass talk. She did obey me; we are no longer going to the village by Piano della Fiera."

The talking she-ass of the Bible stopped in a narrow passage. It had seen the angel of God with the sword.

The she-ass that carried me also stopped—in front of a pool of water that had collected in the mule-track, hollowed out between two huge rocks. I kicked her. She did not move.

"What do you see? Tell me!" I ordered.

I was sure she saw something unusual, like a spirit or an angel. The she-ass of the Bible spoke of what she saw only after a good beating. Should I do the same? No, I decided. I should convince her with good manners.

Once again I asked her why she refused to keep going. I begged her to tell me what she had seen. I was becoming angry. I kicked her hard on her sides; I raised my voice; I yelled. To no avail. As I burst into tears, a man emerged from the bushes at the top of the highest rock to my right. He had a gun. He climbed down towards me.

"A bandit!" I thought.

The first thing that came to my mind was the warning the adults repeated to us children: "If, God forbid, you are ever confronted by one of those men, never say 'I know who you are.' Don't try to be smart. Instead you must repeat, 'I have seen nothing; I have heard nothing; I know nothing.' Do you understand?"

But I remembered that I was Jesus, and one way or another I was going to get out of this situation, even if it took a little miracle. Did I need proof? Here it was.

"Why are you yelling and crying?"

"The she-ass does not want to move on."

"Where are you going?"

"To the village."

"But that's not the way to the village."

"I wanted to go by way of the cemetery."

"What do you have to do in the cemetery?"

"I am Jesus, and I must go there."

"You are Jesus?"

"It's Saint Joseph's Day."

"Oh, I see! So, the she-ass refuses to go on?"

"Yes, sir."

He lifted the tail of the she-ass and kicked her hard: "Come on, get!"

The she-ass did not move. The man took the leather belt from his pants and started beating her on the rear and legs. The pain made her jerk, but she stayed rooted to the spot.

"I know of a sure way to make her go. You, Jesus, stay put right there in the saddle. This works even on oxen and makes them more reasonable when they lie down and won't plow."

He took the candle stub from his haversack, lit it, and placed the flame under the belly of the she-ass. The animal jumped and spun around, but it stayed where it was.

The man asked, "What in the devil does she see? What could it be? She must be afraid of the water, but it's just a puddle. I wonder . . ."

A suspicion came over him, he said, "Let's see. Let's see." He cut a piece of cane and probed the puddle with it.

"How can this be?" he asked in disbelief. The cane went almost completely underwater.

"Go back. Take the road of the Piano della Fiera. This is a big hole, deeper than two meters. Jesus, Jesus! This she-ass has more sense than both of us put together!"

And he left. Before disappearing, he turned around to say, "Give my best to Uncle Luigi."

Uncle Luigi? He knew who I was! So it was true then that my father was friends with everyone, bandits included. It was true that my father had lent his horse to one of them, to Gnazio! What if this man was Gnazio himself? Uncle Luigi was my father, not that there was any real blood tie between the two men, but my father was called "uncle" because in those days in Sicily (and even today in some villages) people thought

of mankind as one big family, all under the same roof. That is why the children called strangers and foreigners "uncles." My father had owned a beautiful horse before it had tumbled down the hill from the village into the creek, cart and all, losing everything we had and leaving us in poverty. One day he had lent it to Gnazio, a bandit who needed to run to his village to see his mother. When the warrant officer who chased the bandit realized that he and his guards, the *carabinieri* (they all rode horses back then), were falling behind, he said, "The only bay horse that could outrun us like that is Luigi's. Let's call him. He has some explaining to do."

My father went to the police headquarters and did not deny that Gnazio had used his horse.

"Why did you lend it to him?"

"I did not lend it to him. I lent it to his mother. I was passing through Barrafranca. Some women asked me to follow them. They took me to Gnazio's mother's house. She was in bed, terribly sick. They begged me to help her son see his mother one last time."

The warrant officer admitted that everything my father said was true.

"But don't try it again, or I will throw you and your horse in jail. When it comes to the law there are no mothers, no fathers and, especially no friends. Remember that!"

Now the pools and puddles on the road made me nervous, and after the *navarrate* (violent downpours brought by the Navarra winds) of the night before, there were many of them. I stopped before a puddle, got off the she-ass, and probed it with an olive shoot I had snatched from the trunk of the nearest tree. The she-ass and I could pass easily. I decided to play a little. In the puddle I saw the reflection of the sky and the clouds, a little bit of the village with the creek, the olive branches, a big bush of prickly pears, the head of the she-ass, and myself, watching it all. I remembered what my mother had said while washing clothes at the *gebbia*. I felt like I was being lifted to the heavens, along with the she-ass, the village, and the prickly pears. I saw—or thought I saw—a circle of light all around my head, and I said to myself, "I have a halo!"

VII

The First Apostle

As I paused on the road to admire the ring of light around my head in the puddle of water, I heard someone sobbing. I stood up to find out what was going on, and I saw a young boy, not much older than me, coming down from the village.

"Where are you going?"

"I don't know. What's it to you?"

"I am Jesus, and I must know everything."

"Which Jesus?"

"The Jesus of Saint Joseph's Day. Do you want to come?"

"I'm going away. I'll never go back to the village again."

"Did they hurt you?"

"Yes."

"Who? Your father? Your mother?"

"Neither. The *carabinieri*."

"The *carabinieri*? Why?"

"Because Montagnese's flock, the flock I worked for, strayed off the path and broke into somebody's vineyard."

"The vines are asleep right now, like the fig trees."

"The farmer chased after us with his gun and killed the dogs. Then the *carabinieri* came. They caught me and the sheep, too. The owner and his sons ran away, and I was the one who got blamed. That's why the *carabinieri* beat me. They said next time they would handcuff me and throw me in jail."

He told me about Montagnese, an outlaw shepherd, and about his sons, who were even worse than their father. Whatever those people spied during the day—firewood, pulleys, jars, the buckets in the wells, plows, and hoes—they would steal at night. They also forced the boy to steal against his will. Anywhere they could not steal, because the flocks were not allowed, they retaliated by setting fires. Montagnese and his sons did what some hunters did in the state forests and the orchards where hunting was forbidden: they burned everything to find where the game was hiding. Once they had located the game, they sent the ferrets to drive it out, and the dogs to chase it. By destroying the vegetation, they even gained access to the orchards where the trees had been bearing fruit before. Some shepherds set fires to the woods and to the fields during the first rains believing that newer, greener pastures would grow from the ashes.

Montagnese burned the haystacks and the crops. He would have set fire to the hut of his own brother, the farmer, if the brother had not warned him of the fate of Abel, or worse. In the Bible we read about Cain the farmer who killed Abel the shepherd. We read how God liked the firstlings of the shepherd's flock more than the first fruit of the farmer's land. We don't read, however, if Abel was a thief and if he was as spiteful as Montagnese; if he ruined his brother's fields with his flock; or if he threw live coals into his crops. We do know that such things were done in America by the so-called cowboys, and also by the Indians of some tribes, hunters, and herdsmen, all of which were the farmers' enemies. My mother remembered reading that the very first men were hunters, then they became shepherds, and finally farmers. Cain went from the plow to commerce. He became a tool and weapons manufacturer, and he built cities. With the coming of industry, we will all become city people, the working masses. After that, no one knows.

The boy's name was Ciccino. He told me about the dogs, all four of them, dead. For a bowl of leftover broth and the whey of ricotta cheese, these dogs were loyal to the flock, like paladins. When the farmer showed up behind the ridge of his field, threatening to shoot shepherds and sheep, Montagnese's sons whistled, and the sheep left the vineyard running. Montagnese's sons, the sheep, and Ciccino ran to safety while the dogs remained behind to stop the farmer. The farmer fired repeatedly, and the dogs fell, one by one.

I thought I had found the first apostle. But I had a problem: Saint Peter was a fisherman. I asked Ciccino, "Have you ever gone fishing in the sea?"

"No. In the river, for eels, but only because they made me."

"From now on you will be Saint Peter."

"Saint Peter? Me?"

"And on this rock I will build my church. I have spoken the sacred words. Now you've got to follow me."

VIII

The Bewildered Man
of the Nativity Scene

Less than an hour after I left on the she-ass, my mother called my father and said to him, "We let our son ride to the village all alone. What about us? Who decided that parents must disappear, that they must stay at home out of sight on the very day their son is chosen to be Jesus? Tradition? Well, a little break from tradition won't hurt. Let's go see if our son got to the church; he should be there by now. The she-ass knows the way, and you said that the flies won't bite. But remember he's just a little boy. What if *he* is the one who gets bitten by the flies? I mean, what if he does something foolish? You have no idea what questions he asked me yesterday! What an imagination! He talked about moving mountains and healing the sick. All from the Gospels, of course, but in the minds of children who believe everything to the letter, it could be trouble. I'm telling you; get the cart ready and let's go to the village."

My father did not agree. He admitted that he felt humiliated and that he could not bear the thought of people pointing and talking about him during the celebration: "Why can't you see that by choosing our son, these people are throwing their pity in our faces?"

My mother replied, "Poverty and hardship have become an obsession with you. What about the children who were chosen before our son? Were they always among the poorest?"

"They sure were, my dear, starting with Jesus Christ himself!"

"All right. Perhaps they were poor, but they were honest and worthy of God's grace, which is the greatest of all riches."

My mother was so unrelenting that my father got the mule out of the stall and hitched it to the cart. And that is how the two of them went to the village, with the mule pulling the cart. They arrived before me, while I was probably still on the road, arguing with the she-ass in front of the puddle of water between the two rocks, or more likely still playing or listening to Ciccino's story. Children have no idea of time. And it was different then; not all people had watches. Now watches are given as gifts to celebrate confirmations and good grades in school. In those days, we kept time according to the sun. But the sky was too big a dial for us to pay too much attention to particular minutes and hours. While the sun was shining, we felt that it was all one hour, one minute, one moment.

Imagine how worried my parents must have been not to find me in the village! Filled with anguish, they went to the parish priest. The priest reassured them, "Don't worry. He will be here. He probably stopped on his way to choose the apostles. But you, why didn't you get the brilliant idea of coming— against tradition, mind you—a little sooner, before your son left on the she-ass all by himself?"

It was getting late, and still no sign of me. The people were coming in and gathering in a little crowd. The priest stood in front of the church, a worried look on his face. Glancing at the church and then at the pocket watch whose chain could be seen through a fold in his black cassock, he fiddled with a small pale-blue tunic for me to wear and the church key he was supposed to give me, not knowing what to do with either of them. On the church square, the number of children wanting to be chosen as saints and apostles kept growing. Saint Joseph, a flowered staff in hand, and Mary, a crown of white flowers on her head, were ready. The priest looked at his watch one more time. Addressing the crowd, he said that if I did not arrive soon, he would choose another Jesus from among the children there. The crowd agreed. My mother tried to say that everyone had to go look for me, that they could not simply ignore how worried she and my father were: "Call the man who plays the drum, the town crier, and let's go look for my son."

"The town crier? But that will put us even more behind! Why don't you go find your son yourself!" yelled someone in the crowd.

There were about ten musicians, all from the neighborhood. They had leaned their instruments against the church wall, waiting to escort the Holy Family to the banquet. They were asked to start playing. The music would be heard in the entire village, Jesus would be alerted, and he would hurry to the church.

When the band started playing, I was with the she-ass and Ciccino under the palm trees of the town hall, very close to the church. I got there so fast that it was like a miracle!

I came with Saint Peter only. That was good news for the children waiting to become saints and apostles. In the joyous confusion, the number of the apostles chosen exceeded the traditional twelve of the Gospels. The priest took it upon himself to impose order as well as the right number. While he was questioning the boys, trying to separate the false saints and apostles from the authentic ones, I heard people whispering:

"We had to wait all this time for him, and he's not even blond! Look at those big lips! He looks like a little African boy!"

"He must have come from the arms of the Lady of Tindari, who is as black as night."

"He looks like u *spavintatu du presepiu* to me."

I too imagined that Jesus was supposed to be fair with blue eyes and golden locks. My hair, grown out again after the typhus, was black and kinky, my eyes were brown, my skin was dark, and I tended to gape at things. My mother was always urging me to close my mouth and not to let things surprise me all the time. I had my mouth open then, but I closed it immediately when I heard them say that I looked like u *spavintatu du presepiu*.

I suppose you would like to know what u *spavintatu* was, and why this term was used to describe people who gaped. *U spavintatu* or *meravigghiatu* means bewildered. It is the name given to a traditional character of the Nativity scene before people started celebrating the birth of Jesus with Santa Claus and the Christmas tree. *U spavintatu* was the first figurine we children looked for, right after the Holy Family, the ox, and the donkey. He stood in front of the cave, to the right of anyone who was looking on. He seemed agitated and excited, filled with a great sense of awe. His eyes, mouth, and arms were wide open. He looked as if he were yelling, speaking about things only he could see. The other characters of the Nativity scene paid him no attention at all. In the fields of moss, by the rivers of silver foil, among the rocks and huts made from the bark of the cork oak, people were walking toward the cave with gifts in their arms, in the same way they would have gone to the wells to draw water or to the market to sell or deliver goods. The shepherds' faces were as expressionless as when they led their herds to the pastures or brought milk to the villages with their goats. The bagpipe player played, the farmer tilled, the bricklayer built a wall, a drinking man drank, and a woman sewed, did dishes, and washed clothes. They were all going about their daily chores as if nothing was happening, as if it were not Jesus who was about to be born in the cave. Only *u spavintatu* was bursting with amazement and wonder, seeing things even the angels could not see.

My mother said that at the moment Christ was born everything froze in time. A man who was walking stopped in his tracks. The air was under a spell, and the birds stopped in their flight. The workers who were lying down around a bowl of soup froze, their fingers still reaching for the food. Those who were eating froze, a piece of soaked bread halfway to their mouths, and those who were drinking froze with a pitcher at their lips. The sheep that were grazing turned to stone. The shepherd who had raised his stick could not bring his arm down. The river stopped flowing, and the lambs froze, their muzzles to the water. My mother believed that there is one moment, every year, when the sun and all things come to a stop, and that is exactly when Jesus was born. This moment when things and people are as still as a photograph is depicted by the Nativity scene and by the paintings and statues we see in church.

When I returned, holding the key and wearing the sky-blue tunic, I thought that almost everyone looked like *u spavintatu* of the Nativity scene. The priest knelt, followed by almost everyone else. I was about to kneel, too, but the priest stopped me, and I remembered that I was the only one who should stand.

We heard the impetuous ringing of the church bells and the explosions of firecrackers. It scared everyone, even the swallows. The smoke and dust made us cough. The musicians struck up a festive march. I entered the church.

IX

Jesus in the Temple

I had asked my mother, and now I was asking myself, "What did Jesus say in the Temple?"

"What do you mean? Don't you know? Even as young as twelve, Jesus talked about things that astounded the teachers of the law. You should know!"

I didn't quite understand what made my mother think that I should know things that even she and other people did not. Could it be that she believed that today I was Jesus, at least a little, and therefore I should have in my mind the words he spoke in the Temple?

We only know Jesus' words from the time he chose the apostles until the Last Supper. We know about what Jesus said to Satan and what Satan said to him during the Temptations. We know of Jesus' suffering, his tears of blood on the Mount of Olives, and his loud cry from the cross just before he died. But of the things Jesus said in the Temple, we don't remember, we haven't written them down, we don't even know a single syllable of them. Do you know why? For the same reason people kept the slab and the pillar on which Jesus, crowned with thorns, was tied up, spat upon, laughed at, and beaten. We have pieces of the cross, the funeral shroud, documents, and exact images of the places where Jesus preached. We know about where and how he got together with the apostles, about the places where he was judged, crucified, and buried. But we do not have a single one of his toys. Think how wonderful it would be if today we could say, "Look, this is the terra cotta whistle that Jesus Christ, the Word of God who came among us, played with when he was little."

My mother could not have answered many of my questions if I had asked her about Adam and Eve when they were children or if there was a time when Cain and Abel played together without fighting too much, not to mention the patriarchs and the prophets! They were all born a hundred years old, long beards and all. Moses must have been a baby, but only so he could be put in a basket and left to float down the Nile. Isaac was a boy so he could test his father Abraham's unconditional obedience to God by his readiness to kill his son. David was a boy so he could kill a man from the next village with a slingshot.

Today the world is full of hugs and kisses. But back then! I remember an uncle of mine, from Calabria, who would boast that he had never held, cuddled or kissed any of his five children! We can understand why in those days people were a little scandalized seeing Jesus hug the children brought to him to be blessed. In the entire Bible, the most renowned kiss is the one Judas gave Jesus, the same night he betrayed him.

We should not be surprised that the evangelists do not tell us about Jesus' childhood, and when they do, they rush through it, passing from one adult to the next: from Zechariah, who heads into prophecy; to Elizabeth, John the Baptist's mother, who feels her baby moving within her; to Mary, who, having received the angel and the Holy Ghost, rejoices, singing, "My soul praises the Lord"; to Joseph, torn by the suspicion that he had been betrayed; to the angel who comes to him in a dream to explain everything. What about the child Jesus? Yes, he is mentioned, but as something precious fallen from the heavens, sent to us to be cherished and placed on the altar, never as a real person, as a child who was alive, who cried, laughed, and played.

People must have started talking about the birth and childhood of Jesus Christ after they saw him perform miracles, especially after the first one, at the wedding in Cana. Changing the water into wine, and what wine! Imagine how surprised those drinking it must have been!

"Who is this man who can do such things?" people must have asked each other, marveling.

"You know, the carpenter's son. Do you remember the baby born in a cave in Bethlehem, when we had to go to the city for the census? Remember the nights we spent in the corral with the animals? Remember how grateful to the Lord we were to find a spot anywhere? When the inns and hostels were full, and we had to pay for water with our blood—not to mention the price of wine? The police and soldiers chasing us everywhere, treating us worse than herds of animals. Do you remember those two? She was very young, riding the donkey, suffering from labor pains; and he was in a daze, walking next to her. And that man who refused to untie the ox from the manger where the child was placed as soon as he was born? And the ox and the donkey breathing on him! Amazing things happened that night. The shepherds talked about wonderful signs. And all those strange people wandering about, more from the other world than from this one, not to mention the crooks! Astrologists and Wise Men came from the East, guided by a special star many people saw shining on Bethlehem. Then came the alarm and sheer terror when people heard that Herod's guards were going around killing babies fresh from the womb. People with small children tried to escape. And the two of them ran away to Egypt. They came back ten or eleven years later for the Easter pilgrimage. Remember the child who puzzled the teachers in the Temple? He must have been the one born in that cave! That must be who he was. The caravan returned home the day after the celebration, his parents thinking he was with them. They traveled the whole day. They were resting when they suddenly realized that their son was missing. Of course, the father thought that he was with his mother, with the women and young children; and the mother thought he was with his father, among the men. But he had stayed behind in the city. They went back, and for three days they looked for him among relatives and friends. Do you know where they found him? He was in the Temple with the teachers who were listening to him in amazement. When his mother and father told him how worried they had been, he answered as if speaking from the chair of Moses: 'Why did you come looking for me? Don't you know that I must be about my Father's business?'" Well, now that we know about all the miracles, we can see his point. But then, if I had been his father and he had sassed me like that, you better believe that no one, not even a prophet, could have saved him from a good whipping!

This preoccupation of mine with what Jesus had said to the teachers did not make much sense. The only thing I was to say in church was "Love ye one another, and I will always be with you," and, "This is how you should pray: 'Our Father who art in Heaven. . . . ,'" and people would follow me in prayer. For the blessing, the priest was supposed to say, "In the name of the Father, and the Son and the Holy Spirit." I only had to raise my hand and make the sign of the cross over everyone.

What about the speech? Better none at all. A few years ago a Jesus before me got all entangled in his words and to untangle himself asked if he could sing a little song. He sang,

> Moon, little moon
> Make me a cakey
> Make it big and good
> I will bring it to Saint Johnny
> If Saint Johnny doesn't want it
> Take it home with you.

Everyone burst into laughter. But the priest and the prominent citizens were not amused. From that year on, the speech was abolished. The reason may have been other than the song. Perhaps people were afraid that children would say things that made no sense, without rhyme or reason—reason, mainly, meaning worldly reason. Jesus, then as when he was alive, young or old, could not say things like "We've had enough with this government!" or "Stop the wars!" Nor could he repeat the curses heard at home against the king of Rome, the head of the government, the ministers, the policemen, and the judges. So, the song got blamed. We knew that song well. We sang it when we walked along the village walls in the moonlight, while the older boys, brooms in hand, had fun knocking down the bats from their niches.

Even without the speech, the phrase "love ye one another" was confusing to me. I could not pronounce "one another" clearly. Wasn't "love ye" enough? What did "I will always be with you" mean? Did it mean that I had to follow everyone, one person at the time, go wherever they went, and do whatever they did, day and night?

I could not grasp the true and real meaning of "Love ye one another." The fact that in the Sicilian dialect the verb *amari* or to love is hardly used did not help me. People used the verb *vuliri beni*, which means to care about someone. *Amari* was used in the popular songs that came from the cities. The songs people sang in the villages, when they were threshing the wheat for instance, said *ti vogghiu beni*, I care for you. They never said *ti amu*, I love you.

I asked, "When do people love one another?"

"When they do good and not evil" was the answer.

"And when do they do good and not evil?"

"When they love one another like Jesus Christ loved us."

Such answers confused me more than Jesus' teachings in the Temple, of which no one remembered a single word. What was even more confusing was going from the language used at home and in church to what people really said and meant. The women would get together in the courtyards to work and chat. They sat in front of their doors while they shelled almonds, cleaned wheat, and sorted chickpeas and lentils, talking aloud and in great detail about everyone's intimate affairs, stopping once in a while to sing popular songs:

> The young maid is crying. Tears of love.
> The young lad does not want her. Wasted tears!

The women with the sharpest tongues were called *curtig-ghiari*, from the word *curtigghiu* meaning "courtyard." Each courtyard had two or three *curtigghiari,* and they were as good as a show. The women would listen to them until they got tired and told the sharp tongues to stop, threatening to go in. At the end of the day, as soon as the bell rang announcing the Ave Maria, the women started reciting the rosary, singing its mysteries. When they finished the prayers, or between mysteries, they would light the fires, call in the children who were playing, and bring the chickens in for the night. One could already hear the shoes of the horses and the donkeys on the cobbled stones, bringing the men from the fields, expecting their dinners.

What was more difficult for us children was to know what fathers, and men in general, thought about love. The men met on the square. They gathered in the taverns and the oil mills, places where women and children were generally not allowed. They met at Chianu, Butera's main square, and sat in a circle, the bills of their caps lowered to their eyes. It looked as if the men were always talking about serious business: work, the land, the animals. Here talk of love would have been out of place. Together, their low voices made an enormous buzz, like many swarms of hornets. At the tavern, the men usually joked and bet for pitchers of wine. It was not unusual at all that they would end up in serious disagreements, such as the one on the eighteenth of March when, for once, my father decided to take me with him . . . and I got slapped. At the wine press and oil mill, the men were funny. They told the most fantastic stories. These were called in fact "wine press tales." There, the men were more crude and gossipy than the *curtigghiari*.

Love, in the church sermons and in my mother's talk, was what Jesus Christ had brought to the world. "Love" and "sacrifice" always went together.

"Love means to care about one another, and to try to do good, through sacrifice. Love, the love everyone talks about, does not amount to a hill of beans if we are not capable of sacrificing ourselves. Mothers and fathers must make sacrifices for the good of their children, the children for the sake of their parents, and all of us for the good of everyone else."

I entered the church feeling awkward in the small pale-blue tunic I was wearing fastened around the waist like a skirt. I was filled with dismay. Was I really going to be able to touch the altar? I went through the communion rail that had always separated us from the priest: the people on one side and the priest on the other with the sacristan, who spent most of the time kneeling down, serving the priest, handing him the water and the wine vials, ringing the bell, and lifting the holy vestment when it was time for the consecration. The priest always kept his back to us. We could not see what he was doing nor understand what he was whispering in that Latin of his, which also seemed to keep its back to the dialect and the language people spoke and understood. At communion, the priest would come down a few steps toward us to give us a broken little host that looked like the scraps of a meal he had eaten all by himself.

I wanted to touch the altar with both hands. Nowadays, children who make their first communion are allowed to take the consecrated host and the cup with their own hands. This is also true for the people who get married, as well as anyone else. In those days, woe to anyone who thought of going where the priest went!

Turning around to face the people, I saw that they were all women. The men were gathered in the back, leaning against the main door. Because of the color of their clothes, they looked like a black cloud of swallows, ravens and crows—the village birds. It was time for me to pronounce the holy words "Love ye one another, and I will always be with you. . . . Pray,

'Our Father who art in Heaven. . . .'" But it was as if I were being carried between the syllables, and a mouth other than mine were speaking those words. In saying what I had to say, I must have waved my arms like someone playing at blind-man's buff. And it was in fearful bewilderment of my entire being that I made the sign of the cross for the blessing.

X

The Three Kings

As we were leaving, amid the ringing of the bells and the explosion of firecrackers, three mysterious characters dressed in old-fashioned clothes appeared outside of the church. They were armed with swords and wore golden crowns on their heads. One of them pulled out his sword and came towards me. We heard a faint chorus of voices behind him: "Pray, stop thy barbarian hand!"

He put the sword back in its sheath, and he and his two other companions vanished.

Years later, when I inquired in Butera about the whereabouts and the identity of those three people, I was given the following explanations: "Three people with swords, waiting for you outside the church? I have never seen them. Never heard of them. You must have made them up for your story."

Or: "They were the Wise Men, but they had nothing to do with the feast of Saint Joseph. They only came at Christmas time and never as human beings. They were puppets, small terra cotta statues."

Or: "Yes, they were the Wise Men. They were made of sugar. I bought them myself in Caltagirone. They were for All Souls' Day, not for Saint Joseph."

And: "What are you talking about? The Wise Men in Butera for the nineteenth of March? You are confusing our village with another that has the custom you are talking about; there are some in central Sicily, I believe."

Finally, my cousins Maria and Franca cleared it up: "It may be that the feast in Butera was celebrated that year according to the custom of the village that paid for the banquet, in fulfillment of a vow. Their tradition must have included the Wise Men, like in our village, Pietraperzia.

"The band that accompanied you from the church to the Castle was probably hired by an outsider. In Butera, they only have the town crier and his drum, and a couple of other musicians at most."

That would explain why some people and the chorus that sang out, "Pray, stop thy barbarian hand" were not from Butera. We could tell where a person was from just by listening to the way he or she pronounced certain syllables or used the article *"lu"* instead of *"u."* My father, who was from Riesi, said *"lu pani, lu vino"* for "the bread, the wine." My mother who was from Butera said *"u pani, u vino."* People from Caltagirone, said and still say *"u uàni, u uìnu."* They nasalize all the words in a play of vowels as if they were about to yawn with a mouth full of beans. But even my cousins could not tell me who and what those three individuals were supposed to be. Had they been the Wise Men, they should have come to greet me with gifts instead of swords. The chorus sang a long stanza that neither I nor my cousins remembered. The only thing I do remember

68

is that first line and the gesture one of them made when he put the sword back in its sheath.

Someone who thinks he knows a lot maintains that the three kings were those of the constellation which appeared very early in the morning when the men got ready to leave on their horses and donkeys. The three men came in front of the *Puddhara,* the polar star. But it could have been Sirius or another star since in those days farmers and shepherds saw many more stars than we do today.

The priest (a new one, because the old one has already gone to have questions of this sort cleared up for him in Heaven) thinks that people mixed up the Wise Men with the soldiers Herod sent to kill Baby Jesus. And really, aside from the golden crowns, the three of them did look like Roman soldiers. Maybe Herod's guards arrested the Wise Men on their way back to their villages. When they turned them over to Herod, he must have said to the Wise Men, "I told you to come back here before returning to your villages. I begged you to tell me where I could find the child who is to become the King of Kings so that I, too, could go adore him. Instead, here you are, caught sneaking away like thieves. Good thing I had you followed by my men! That's how I know you found the child and brought him presents."

That said, Herod had the Wise Men killed, dressed his soldiers in their clothes, and ordered them to get rid of the child Jesus. But, either because they were touched and moved to pity when they arrived in front of the cave or because the crowd of people (among which were very strong shepherds and Bedouins) intimidated them, the soldiers, one of whom had already pulled out his sword, changed their minds and let things go the way it was written and was supposed to happen.

If the Wise Men had returned to their own villages, they would have spoken about what they had seen. But in the East where they are from, people never heard anything at all.

When the incident with those three individuals was over, I hugged the Virgin Mary and Saint Joseph. The Holy Family, the saints, and the apostles, accompanied by the music, were on their way to the Castle.

Butera's Castle, while very old, was no fairy tale castle. In fact, the prison was there, between the mill, the pasta factory, and the convent. Everywhere in the world, the concept of going up means to reach a more beautiful and better place in life, to escape from the slavery and chains below. In Butera, it was the opposite. People who misbehaved heard threats such as: "If you don't change, you'll go straight up to the Castle, behind bars, like the goldfinch in the pharmacist's cage."

Or: "Go on up, up, on your way to the Castle, you fool! As for us, we are going down, thank God."

Since the entire village was built up, like the tower of Babel, people used to say of anyone who went there on a good deed—the bishop of Piazza Armerina or perhaps a doctor from Syracuse or Agrigento—that the man of God had made "the sacrifice of coming up to our place," where even the ravens and the crows refused to go. The birds, the strongest ones included, remained in the cove, circling in the sky under the walls where they nested. They never flew farther up. Perhaps it was because there was no food for them to eat or because they were afraid of becoming food for others. The naive swallows arrived just about the time of the celebration we are talking about. Their nests, built under the gutters, were often destroyed pulled down with long sticks. The baby swallows did not stand a chance. They fell, featherless and peeping, while their mothers dove like arrows, shrilling and skimming the ground. When the game and the misery were over, the dead little birds could be seen in some corner, being devoured by the ants.

"Don't look at your feet all the time!" was another of my mother's admonishments, like her urging me to keep my mouth closed. So I looked up, ahead of me, towards the Castle while the band played on. I imagined that through the bars of the grated windows of the dungeon I would see the waving of hands and the glow of the prisoners' faces. But they would be happy, like the swallows that are able to forget the abuse of the nests and fly between the roofs, friendly and happy once again. That day, "going up" could have a different meaning. Of course, it would mean forgiveness and freedom for the people behind bars but also much more, since I had not abandoned the idea of performing a miracle.

Like many other castles, Butera's had its prisoners, human beings totally cut off from life, imprisoned there for hundreds of years. There was also a big treasure. During the night, lost souls came knocking at the villagers' dreams. One of them came to my mother. He told her that he had been in the service of a prince (she could read about him in the town's archives) and that he had been killed and buried with a treasure in the Castle. In order to free his soul and get to the treasure, my mother, the prison guard, and an unfortunate woman whom he named, must go to the Castle on an odd-numbered day as soon as the sun came out. The spirit added that immediately upon awakening from her dream, my mother would see a dove fly into a room of the Castle. The three of them, careful not to wear any pins or needles on their clothing, should go to that room and each eat a forkful of pasta cooked without salt. At that point three bricks would cave in, and there they would find the treasure, a treasure so huge that it would make them very rich even if they had to give the government its share. When my mother woke up, she prepared to go to the Castle, which was located near our old house. Outside, as if waiting for her, a dove took flight and flew through a window of the Castle. My mother went to the prison guard and said to him: "Godfather, tomorrow we can change our station in life."

She told him about the dream and about the dove she had just seen fly into the room. The guard sighed and said, "Godmother." We must remember that in those days, people were not only all related to one another, but they were also godfathers and godmothers and godchildren, in the name of Saint John the Baptist, whose very sacred and respected ties extended way further than baptism and first communion. This was celebrated in many ways, like when the children cut the petals of carnations and put them in each other's hair.

"Godmother," repeated the guard, "this job was given to me by the government. It is my only daily bread. I don't want to lose it."

The following night, my mother saw her now-familiar spirit in a dream. He said to her, "I am really sorry for you, but he will lose the job he was so afraid for and everything else."

A little while after, two prisoners escaped from the Castle and the guard got fired.

My mother thought there were many treasures hidden in the Castle and that they remained buried or turned to dust and ashes like the bones of the unfortunate people who lay with them because of men's stupidity and lack of courage. She thought that it would never be possible to find them unless the instructions she had received in her dream were scrupulously followed. "It's like trying to open a lock with the wrong key or taking one medicine for another, when and how we choose to do it, in total disregard for science. The prison guard was so dumb, he started laughing when he heard that we had to eat a forkful of pasta cooked without salt. I told him, 'My dear godfather, making fun of dreams that can open our minds and our eyes to so many things means that you have neither imagination nor common sense. Let me remind you, my dear godfather, that it is through dreams that God himself talked with the angels, the prophets, and the saints, starting with Saint Joseph, whose name you bear. I know that certain things may seem absurd, but then everything is absurd in religion and science. It is absurd to plow and to sow, to expect to see spears grow through grass and flowers become fruit. The forkful of pasta cooked without salt is probably some sort of password that the spirit, like a sentry placed between this world and the other, has to obey and make us obey. What about you, my dear godfather, don't you have your own secret sign that binds you, the prison guard, to the prisoner you must look after?'"

While we followed the road along the walls of San Rocco, up the hill toward the Castle, I asked myself if it would not be enough to eat a forkful of pasta with honey—customary for Saint Joseph—to free the lost souls and discover the treasure. Saints and apostles would dip their hands into the jars full of gold coins, distributing all that wealth to the people I was blessing. The words "saint and rich" would finally become true for everyone. Those were the words used by our parents and adults when they answered the children's greeting "Please bless us."

As long as the band played, the miracle seemed possible. Once the band stopped, and I found myself surrounded by the sounds and the voices of the people, doubts overcame me. Thank heavens the town crier started playing the drum again. It was better than nothing, and it kept my dreams alive.

XI

The Saints at the Table

On the eve of the feast, the children sang,

> Belly of mine, become a big pouch
> Tomorrow is Saint Joseph's Day!

The feast was mainly about food. Adults and children forced themselves to fast before the feast to make sure they would be very hungry and be able to cram everything into their big pouch of a belly. In those days, the prayer "Our Father, who art in Heaven. . . . Give us this day our daily bread," reflected the daily struggle to find enough to eat. On Tuesdays, Saint Anthony's devotees sang in prayers:

> Saint Anthony, at all hours
> In plague and in hunger. . . .

Much more than the plague, which came only once in a while, it was hunger that made the world suffer. It should not be a surprise, therefore, that when some degree of prosperity reached our small towns and villages shortly after World War

II, people took to eating and drinking and taking tons of medicine for all the hunger and illnesses of the past. Everyone put on a little belly, and many got sick from having cured themselves of the plagues and the ills that had afflicted their fathers and forefathers. In Sicily, to this day, God forbid that anyone should turn down an invitation to drink or eat! A guest is a being of thirst and hunger who must be fed and restored.

Children were mouths to feed. To save money mothers kept them suckling at their breasts until they were two years old, even older. We read that Bovo d'Antona, a hero in the Epics of France, nursed until he was seven years old. Perhaps it is because of the great hunger that has plagued humankind that Jesus Christ made himself food and drink—of eternal life, of course. By doing so he answered the fundamental need of all human beings who, especially so long ago, must have been like hungry and needy children, touching and bringing everything to their mouths. Hunger has not disappeared. In countries like ours it has simply moved from our stomachs to other parts of our bodies and minds. This is why we are called consumers, as if we devour it all, from books to cars, to our enemies, to life itself.

My sister Gina, who studied at the convent near the Castle, says that the women had the pasta and the honey ready two weeks before the feast day: twenty kilos of honey, fifty kilos of pasta, and the bread, already toasted and grated into crumbs. They cooked the pasta just at the right moment in the courtyards on the day of the nineteenth, in the huge pots used for making tomato paste and for cooking the wine.

We could hear the ringing of bells and the firecrackers early in the morning. Some shots were fired as we left the church. As we approached the Castle, rosary after rosary of firecrackers erupted on the side of the road until one huge explosion deafened the saints and apostles and terrified our shy little Madonna, who was always on the verge of tears anyway.

The table was set in the big room of the mill. The machines, idle and covered with oilcloths, looked like the big crucifixes that are veiled in church during Lent. Lighted candles and flowers made a rustic and informal altar. The food we were supposed to eat was nowhere in sight. The anticipation of beholding food and eating could be seen in the eyes of the saints and the non-saints, eyes that were searching everywhere for all the good things of God at the banquet.

I must say that in the country, we children did not go hungry. Aside from the fact that we never lacked for bread, as my father had so proudly pointed out, we could eat all kinds of food: garden vegetables, eggs, milk, and venison, which was plentiful then. And in fruit season I spent my time eating from tree to tree: an apple or two here; half a pear there, the other half for the wasps and the ants; a bunch of carnelian grapes; the first mature pomegranate that fell open at my feet; some walnuts which, in a bet with myself, I felled from the tree with a stone; then I'd go down to the spring to sip its fresh water through a straw of cane. My mother made sure that I did not fast the day before. She simply advised me not to eat too much in the morning since I had to do justice to the meal.

The prayer which started the banquet sounded loud and solemn among the ghostly covered machines of the mill. The first dishes appeared suddenly: small and glittering dishes of orange slices seasoned with cinnamon and pepper. We would have a taste only, as was the custom. And then, out of the dark corners of the room, propelled by a huge collective sigh, came the big pots of pasta and honey. Plates and orange slices flew away, disappeared. They did not have to tell us, "Our Lord, our Lady, Saint Joseph, please eat." A hunger, I had no idea where

it came from, took over and satisfied, without a doubt, the expectations of anyone looking for signs of grace in Jesus' good appetite. After cleaning our plates of pasta and honey, we ate, in the traditional order:

Rice with milk

Omelets

Ricotta and egg frittatas

Small curly fennels, pan fried

Roasted almonds and candied chickpeas

Regular fennels, raw

The women served water and wine, constantly encouraging us, "Eat and drink, my Lord. Eat and drink, my Lady. Eat and drink, Saint Joseph. And have mercy on us!"

Our mothers urged us not to drink wine; we should only taste it and then drink water.

I was shocked to see the musicians eating among the machines and piles of sacks. Spaghetti with tomato sauce had been prepared for them as well as for the other men; the women, on the other hand, ate pasta with honey as we children did. The fact that the musicians ate was odd to me. I was so used to seeing them with trumpets and flutes, as if music were the only relationship between them and the world. But even stranger to me was that the municipal guard also ate. So, under the cap with the eagle representing the law, was hair and the pale forehead of a man! It was amazing because some people, like puppets in a show, did not seem to have the weakness of eating. I did understand that a French paladin could be killed, but I could not for the life of me imagine him behind closed doors, swallowing forkfuls of spaghetti and drinking wine!

We had gotten to the almonds and the chickpeas when a woman burst into the room. All dressed in black, disheveled and barefoot, she started screaming and pulling out her hair, weeping for her dying daughter. People grabbed her and took her away. It was Rocchina, the madwoman. Her daughter had died years ago, but she continued to grieve for her every day as if at every moment her daughter were still at the point of death. Rocchina's lamentations could still be heard even as the saints bit into the raw fennels served at the end of the banquet. The Madonna, whose black eyes squinted a little, started to cry; Saint Joseph next and then some other children broke into tears. I tried to control myself, but a tear blurred my sight and made the flames of the candles flicker in front of me. I washed it down, salted as it was, with a sip of wine.

XII

Judas

In the early afternoon of the feast, the village gave itself and the children a few hours of rest and play while the women cleared the tables and prepared new dishes for supper. Our little Madonna and her friends stayed on the steps in front of a closed door to play and talk about all the wonderful things we had eaten at lunch while the boy saints went running along the village walls. What we really wanted to do was throw rocks down the cliffs and slide down the gullies beside the convent among the garbage and the carcasses of the dead animals. We would have liked to shoot our slingshots and fling stones at the nests between the battlements of the Castle, but wise voices told us that we should not do such things now, especially on the day we were given saints' names. Saint Joseph, who was a little older than the rest of us, decided wisely to take home the sesame seed bread and all the other gifts he had received during the banquet. I, too, had been given a sesame seed loaf shaped like a rooster, which I carried in my arms. I did not know where to take it. Our house in the country was too far away, and the she-ass was probably with my father and mother, who had vanished before I went into the church. With a full stomach, one is not really interested in performing miracles; one does not see the need. Besides, Rocchina's screams had shaken my confidence.

So I went to Uncle Liborio's. He was a friend of my father's who had been blinded by lime. He lived nearby, between the Castle and the village walls. But I could not bring him the bread shaped like a rooster! What I needed was a little keg of wine like the one my father usually sent him. But where in the world were my father and mother?

Uncle Liborio ("uncle" because, once again, everyone is related in the villages) was in an empty stall built partly in the hill, weaving baskets in the dark. Outside the entrance, the tips of three strips of reed could be seen skipping about, slowly getting shorter as the man's fingers wove them into a basket.

"*Vossia benedica.* Good afternoon."

"Who are you?"

"I am Jesus and I am bringing the sesame seed bread."

"Yes, I see you."

"You see me?"

"Sure I see you."

"I thought you couldn't see."

"Who told you such a silly thing? I can see. But there isn't enough light for my eyes."

"The sun is shining outside."

"The sun won't do anymore. Do you understand?"

I did not understand. I left him to go visit Nico. Nico lived with his aunt on a side street, to the left, down Via San Rocco. His aunt took care of him and had promised to get him a small job one day with the village carpenter or with the barber. His parents lived in the country, beyond the river's bank, on the way up to Cadauru's bridge. Short and chubby, with an olive-yellow complexion, sitting on a stool, elbows on an over-turned kneading trough, Nico was staring at a glass of water and at a pill, every kid's nightmare. His aunt was begging him and threatening him with the worst—death itself—if he did not take it.

"Here is Jesus, here is Jesus! You! You tell him to take the pill!" said the aunt when she saw me.

I asked if he had malaria. No, that's not what it was, it was not the season for it yet. It was worms or something else. No matter—the quinine pill was good for everything; that's what people believed. Personally, I thought that illnesses were like fruit, each coming in its own season, and many during the summer when children and adults alike suffered from malaria. As for Nico, he must have had an orchard full of illnesses.

How dreadful were those worms living in our bellies! With no warning at all they made a child turn white, fall on the ground, eyes wide open, and kick his little legs like a rabbit with a fatal blow to the back of its head. That is why sometimes we could hear mothers screaming all over the neighborhood. My mother knew how to *giarmàrli,* how to "call" the worms by massaging the child's infested stomach and whispering prayers. She got credit for having saved the life of more than one child. We were warned not to chew or suck on the roots of licorice. Sweetness woke the worms up and bitterness calmed them down. During the grape harvest, because of the sweetness of the grapes, they even went after the adults. Some died. In spite of all the warnings, we had fun digging up the little plants of licorice. I remember our delight when the long roots would come up at the first pull, and our disappointment, our boasts,

83

how hard we tried until our hands hurt when the plant held firmly in the ground and refused to come out.

Nico looked sad, his eyes on the round little pill. One could have said that he was a poor Christ, silently saying to himself, "If possible, take away this bitter pill from me!" For they were bitter—really bitter, those quinine pills—as anyone who took them can attest.

"I brought you the sesame seed bread."

"The bread is yours. You must take it home. We can't accept it," said Nico's aunt, who as we have already seen did not bother to call me my lord. She was a seamstress and was not overly religious. But she was right; I should take home my sesame seed bread shaped like a rooster. Our Lady took hers, which looked like a dove, and Saint Joseph his—a big long loaf in the shape of a flowering staff.

Still staring at the pill, Nico took a deep breath and said "You make me a saint?"

"Who do you want to be?"

"Saint Bartholomew."

"The patron saint of country fairs? Why?"

"I like it."

"We already have one."

"Who can I be then?"

"The only one we don't have is Judas."

"No, I don't want to be Judas. Wait, OK, I'll be Judas but without the betrayal. Just to be with you and the others."

"OK. To be together."

And down went the pill.

XIII
And So the Story Ends . . .

The town crier with his drum made his round, to call back the saints and the apostles for supper. It was the hour of the Ave Maria, the hour when the women began reciting the rosary in the courtyards. The mysteries contemplated that day were joyful. Anyone who felt an excess of fervor could go on reciting the Glorious Mysteries, skipping the Sorrowful Mysteries except when there were strong reasons for mourning.

The drum led us directly to the Castle without the musical band or firecrackers. In the big room of the mill some of the oilcloths were missing. They had fallen on the ground or had been removed, and wheels and machine belts were sticking out. For supper the orange slices seasoned with cinnamon and pepper reappeared, but no pasta with honey followed, and there was no bread. We had beans, artichokes, and dried salted cod. And although the familiar "eat and drink" refrain of the women could still be heard, it lacked the spirit of the luncheon. The curly little fennels showed up again. The men were nowhere to be seen, and only a third of the women who had served us lunch were there. No one was expecting grace or miracles from us. The spirit of the prayers had been exhausted or was about to embark upon new relationships that had nothing to do with us. We had done our job, and for that year we were no longer mediators between Heaven and Earth. Soon we would be guilty again of not understanding, of not working, of being mouths to feed. Someone would throw the celebration in our faces, reproaching us as unworthy of the name and of the task that had been given to us this day.

At a certain moment when even the women had vacated the room leaving us by ourselves, we looked at each other, and for no reason at all, we burst into laughter.

The women and a few men returned. With a puzzled expression on their faces, they looked and gestured towards one another, finally asking, "Why are you laughing? What happened? What did you see? What's the matter with you?"

Instead of answering, we laughed even harder, and because the laughter we felt was so powerful, some of us stamped our feet, others clapped their hands, others snorted, others held their sides, and others did many other things.

"They are laughing with the angels!" That's what they said in Sicily when a child laughed by himself. But there were so many of us! Forget the angels! It could be said that we were laughing with God or, as the rumor spread among the grown-ups, that we were drunk. The women ran to check our glasses; some glasses had been emptied. The first one to be called was our Lady.

"Our beautiful Lady, you drank a whole glass of wine!"

The tiny coals of the squinting little eyes shone with a light never seen before. The little mouth without teeth opened only to give way to other waves of laughter, so many missing teeth in happiness!

A girl about twelve or thirteen years old, my sister Gina's age, left the room and ran into the street yelling, "The saints got drunk! The saints got drunk!" She was the last one to call us saints, the others went back to calling us "little ones," "darling," and "mamma's baby."

The news that the children had gotten drunk spread at once. Mothers and fathers rushed to their children. Some got angry at the women who had left us. We should have been supervised! No one thought of criticizing the tradition of irresponsibly serving liquor to grown-ups and children alike during the celebrations. I remember how my one-and-a-half-year-old little nephew Luigino was given a glass of liquor at a christening—strong liquor at that. The little boy drank it and then cried. And what about the people in the south who give their children wine instead of milk, and those in the north who give them beer? Don't they all boast about it?

I don't think we were drunk. We drank so little. Except perhaps for our Lady, although she had spilled a lot of her wine on the table. The only one who could have been a bit tipsy was Judas. Even though he had swallowed the pill, his aunt had done all she could to keep him at home. But when Nico heard the town crier's drum, he left the house and joined us at the Castle. Using a blanket as a cape, Nico came into the room and said very seriously, "I am Judas. Make room for me."

He sat at Saint Peter's side and was given a plate and a glass. A woman asked him how he was doing.

"Not too well, but I'll feel better after some wine."

He drank and then explained that his father used wine to chase away malaria, colds, and worms.

The fact was that Nico was the one who was laughing the most. His blanket fell on the floor.

My father and mother reappeared with the cart. They took me with them, my little tunic and all. I did not stop laughing even when I was on the cart with them.

"Could we know what happened?"

The questions made me laugh even more. Not wanting to be rude to my parents, I tried to answer, "Nothing, nothing!"

"You must have gotten into some kind of trouble," said my father.

"No. Nothing."

"Then it's true that you did have wine. You got drunk."

"We didn't drink. Only Judas and the Lady. Me, just a little at noon and almost nothing at supper."

"But surely something happened!"

"And what do you think happened?" said my mother. "For children, laughing and crying is the same thing. Sometimes there is no reason at all, and if there is one, it is unknown to us and to themselves."

"Where is the she-ass?" I asked.

"She went back to the herd by herself," was the answer given to me by my father or mother, I don't remember which. Because of the laughter I felt coming again and because of the noise made on the rocky road by the cart wheels and the mule's hooves, their voices came to me one and the same.

We were going down toward the valley. Now that the wheels had left the big road and rolled quietly on the sandy cartway, I began feeling tired and sleepy. It was getting dark. My father stopped the cart and, like the evening before, got off to put on the light.

"You are not laughing anymore?" he asked me as he climbed back to his seat.

I was no longer laughing. Resting against a half-full sack of wheat behind my parents, who sat with their legs dangling between the cart shafts and the tail of the mule, I was thinking, pondering the meaning of "one another." I was now confusing in my mind the stars and the lights of the village we had left behind as well as the scattered fires people had lit in the countryside. The sky and the earth were a single night. And in that night our mule was going forward, tenaciously, a light swinging between the wheels of the cart that carried us.

"My sweet Little Jesus, go to sleep!" whispered my mother, covering me with her shawl.

That was the last time I was called by his holy name, and I fell asleep, filled with thoughts of Him.